Date Due

[illegible]	FEB 27 2018		
2-2			
12-15			
1-8			
OCT 25 2005			
FEB 27 2006			
OC 09 '11			

Modern Curriculum Press
BEGINNING TO READ Series

The Yellow Boat

Library of Congress Catalog Card Number: AC 66-10515

Hillert, Margaret.
The yellow boat.

ISBN 0-8136-5533-1 Paperback
ISBN 0-8136-5033-X Hardbound

2 3 4 5 6 7 8 9 10 88 87 86 85

The Yellow Boat

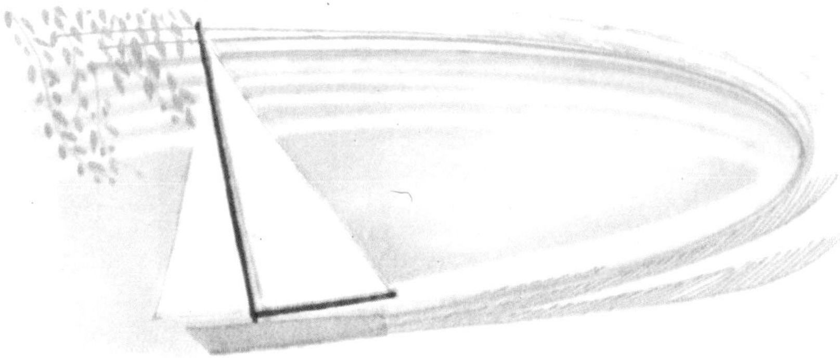

Margaret Hillert

Illustrated by Ed Young

MODERN CURRICULUM PRESS
Cleveland • Toronto

Look here, look here.

See the little boat.

A little yellow boat.

The boat can go.

It can go away.

Go, little boat, go.

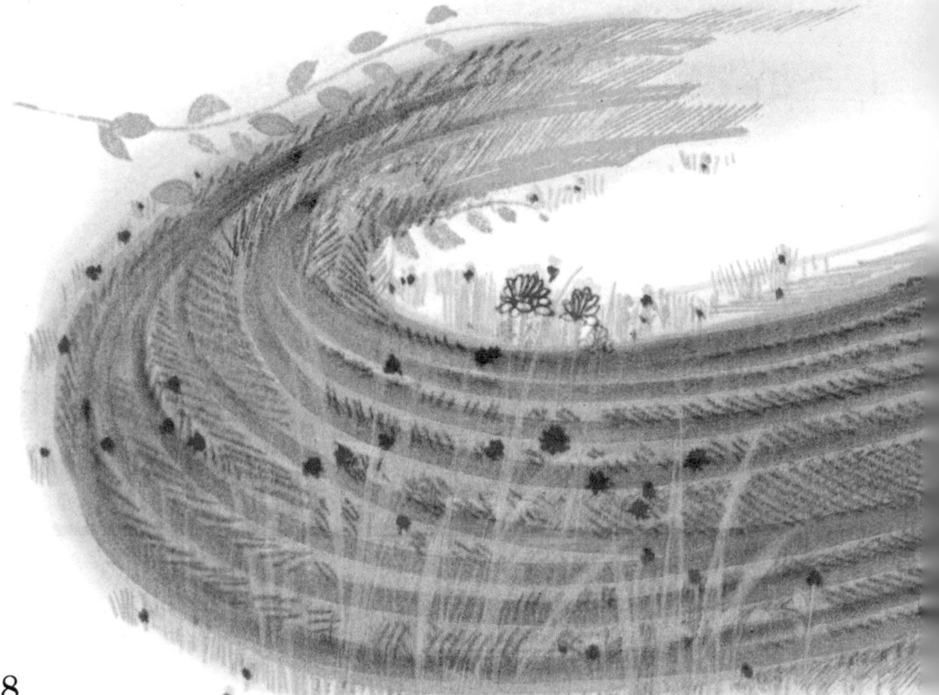

Away, away.

The boat can go away.

Oh, look, look.

Here is something.

It is funny.

Oh, my.

It can jump.

See it jump.

Jump, jump, jump.

Oh, oh, oh.

Something big is here.

Big, big, big.

Can it jump?

It can not jump.

It can go down, down, down.

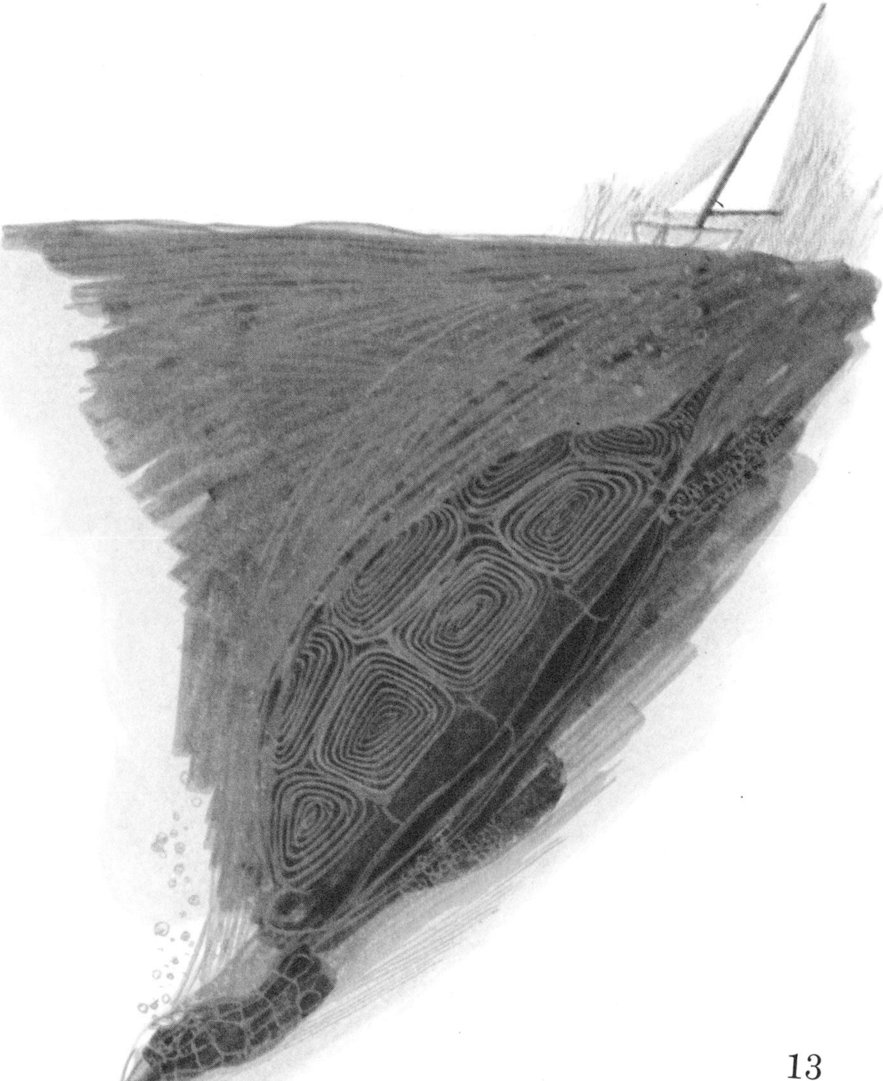

Look here, look here.

One little one.

Two little ones.

Three little ones.

Where is the boat?

Where is it?

Find the little boat.

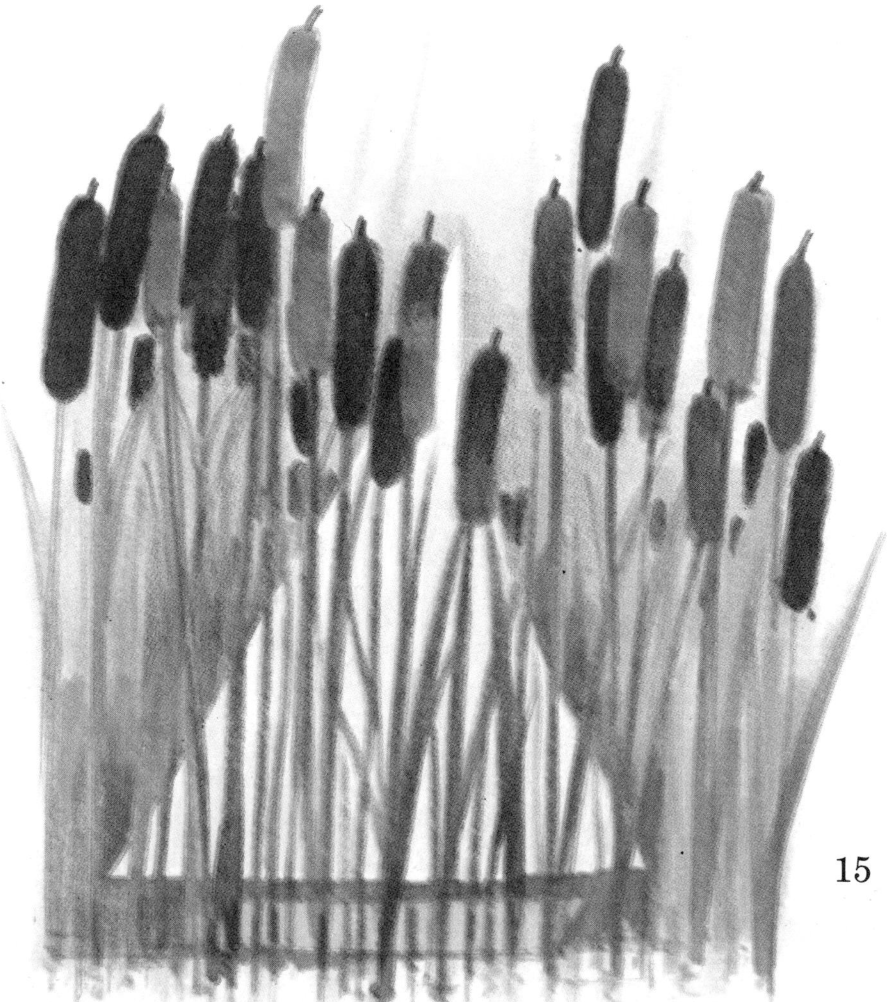

Oh, here it is.

Here is the yellow boat.

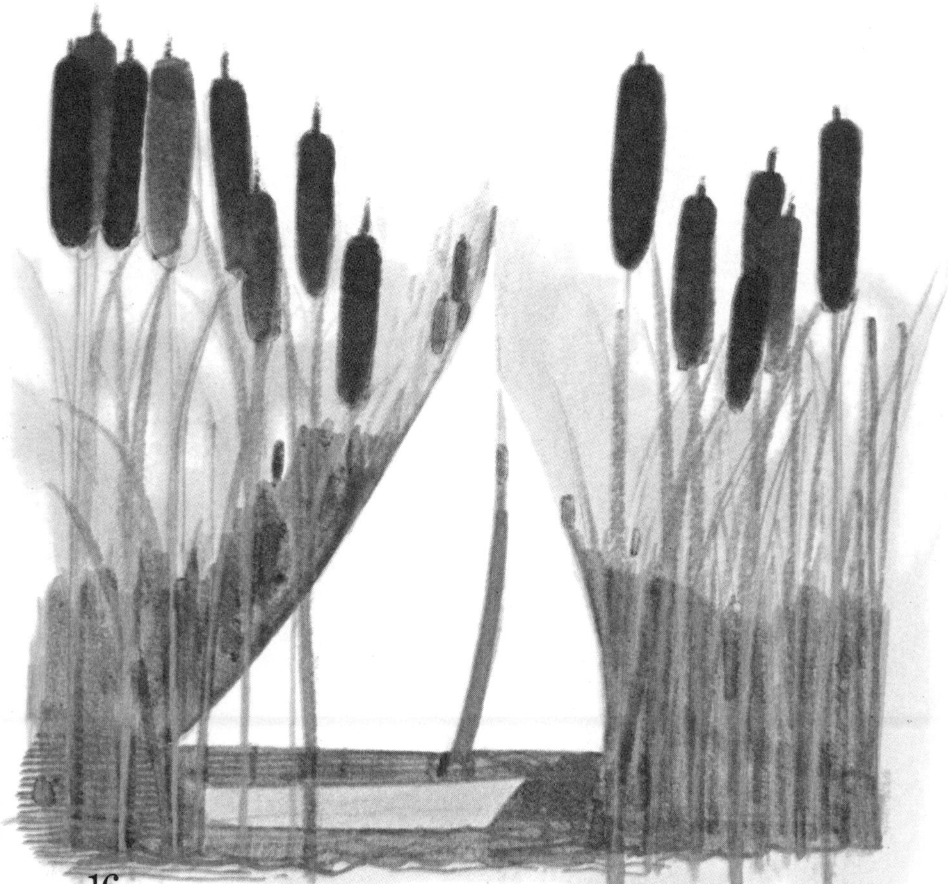

Go, boat, go.

Go away, away.

Here is something little.

It is blue.

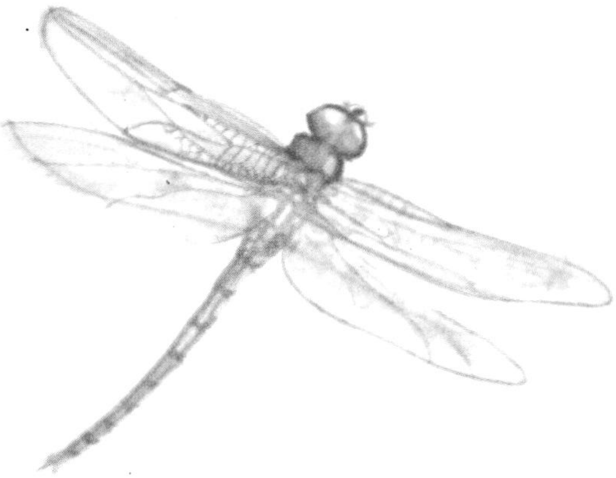

It can go up.

Up, up, up and away.

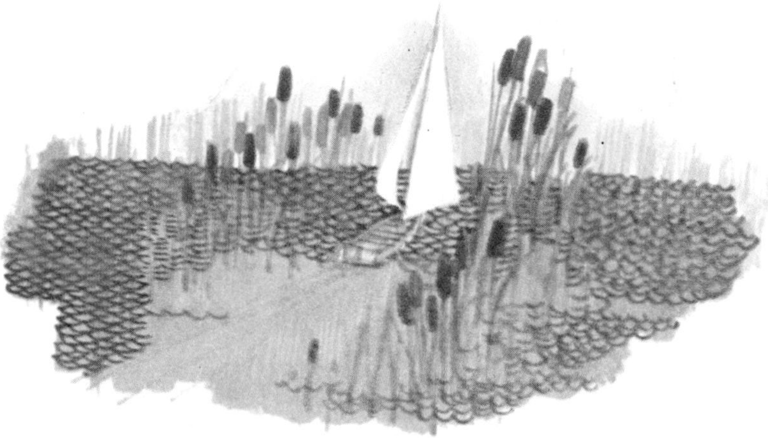

Here is a mother.

Here is a baby.

A little yellow baby.

Look, look.

See the baby play.

And here is something funny.

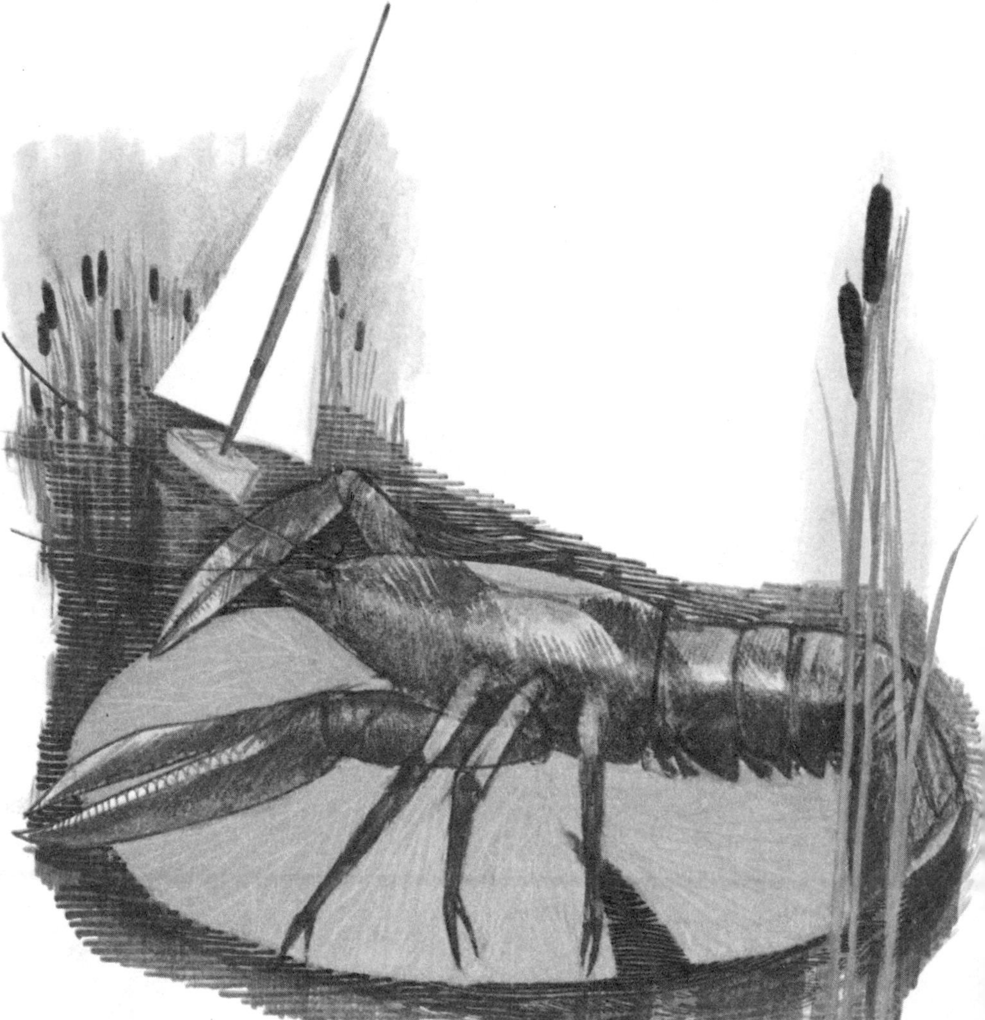

Help, help.

Go away, go away.

You make me want to run.

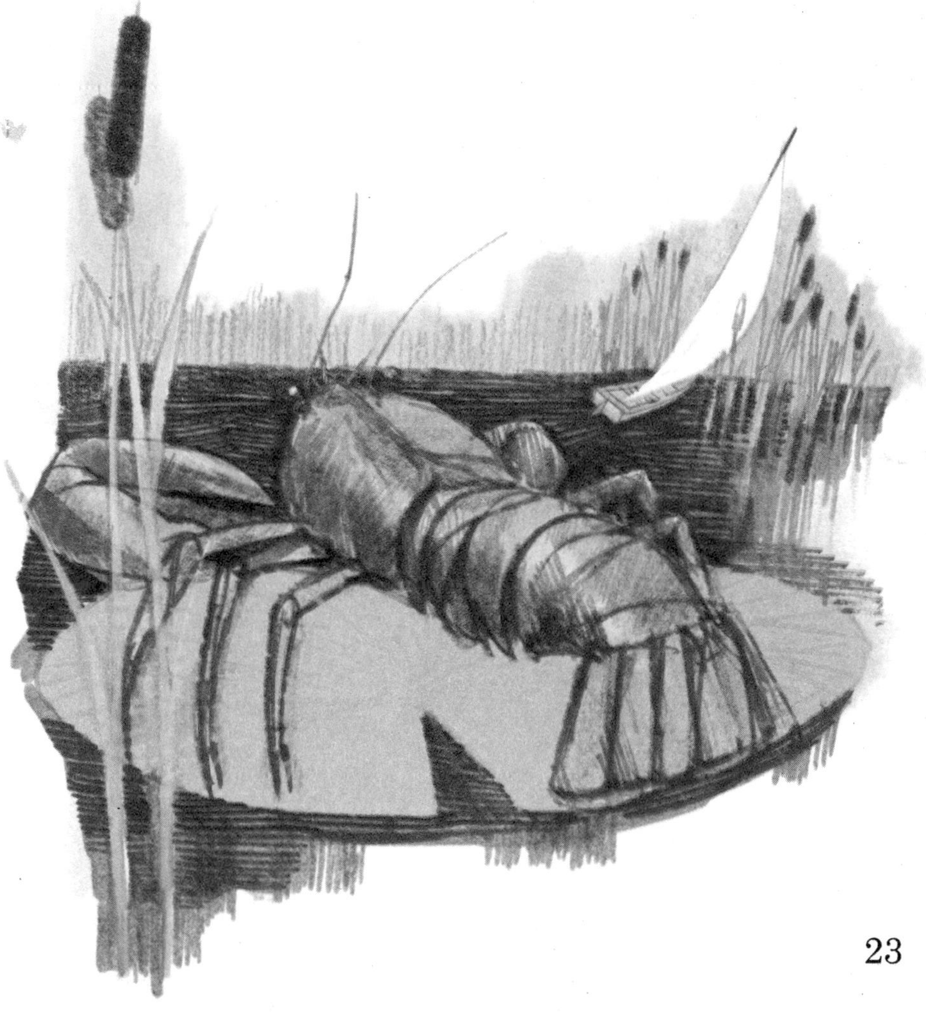

Here comes something.

I see something little.

Oh my, oh my.

It is a little yellow boat.

See the yellow boat.

Oh, yellow boat.

I want you.

I want you.

Come to my house.

Here you go.

In here, in here.

Go, yellow boat, go.

Follett JUST Beginning-to-Read Books

Uses of these books. These books are planned for the very youngest readers, those who have been learning to read for about six to eight weeks and who have a small preprimer reading vocabulary. The books are written by Margaret Hillert, a first-grade teacher in the Royal Oak, Michigan, schools. Each book is illustrated in full color.

Children will have a feeling of accomplishment in their first reading experiences with these delightful books that *they can read.*

The Yellow Boat

Children will enjoy the adventure of the yellow boat which is charmingly illustrated and uses just 43 preprimer words.

Word List

7 look
here
see
the
little
boat
a
yellow
8 can
go
it
away
10 oh
is
something
funny
11 my
jump
12 big
13 not
down
14 one
two
three
15 where
find
18 blue
19 up
and
20 mother
baby
21 play
23 help
you
make
me
want
to
run
24 comes
I
26 house
27 in